· Gordon ·

· Harold ·

· Percy ·

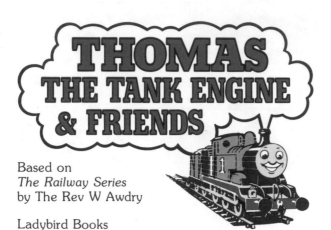

THOMAS THE TANK ENGINE & FRIENDS

Based on
The Railway Series
by The Rev W Awdry

Ladybird Books

Acknowledgment
*Photographic stills by David Mitton and Terry Permane
for Britt Allcroft Ltd.*

British Library Cataloguing in Publication Data

Awdry, W.
    Pop goes the diesel; Dirty work; A close shave.—
    (Thomas the tank engine and friends; 11)
    I. Awdry, W.   II. Series
    823'.914[J]   PZ7
    ISBN 0-7214-1030-8

Pop goes the diesel

Pop goes the diesel

Duck is very proud of being Great Western. He talks endlessly about it. But he works hard too and makes everything go like clockwork.

Today it was a splendid day on the Island of Sodor. The trucks and coaches were behaving well, and the passengers had stopped grumbling! But the engines didn't like having to bustle about.

"There are two ways of doing things," Duck told them. "The Great Western way, or the wrong way. I'm Great Western and..."

"Don't we know it," the engines groaned.

James, Gordon and Henry were glad when a visitor came. He purred smoothly towards them.

The Fat Controller introduced him. "Here is Diesel," he said. "I have agreed to give him a trial. He needs to learn. Please teach him, Duck."

"Good morning," purred Diesel in an oily voice. "Pleased to meet you, Duck. Is that James – *and* Henry – *and* Gordon, too? I am delighted to meet such famous engines."

The silly engines were flattered. "He has very good manners," they murmured to

each other. "We are very pleased to have him in our yard."

Duck had his doubts. "Come on," he said, impatiently.

"Ah yes!" said Diesel. "The yard, of course. Excuse me, engines."

Diesel purred after Duck, talking hard. "Your worthy Fat..."

"Sir Topham Hatt to you," ordered Duck.

Diesel looked hurt. "Your worthy Sir Topham Hatt thinks I need to learn. He is mistaken. We diesels don't need to

learn. We know everything. We come to a yard and improve it. We are revolutionary."

"Oh!" said Duck. "If you're revo-thingummy, perhaps you would collect my trucks while I fetch Gordon's coaches."

Diesel, delighted to show off, purred away.

When Duck returned Diesel was trying to take some trucks from a siding. They were old and empty. They had not been touched for a long time. Diesel found them hard to move.

Pull – push – backwards – forwards.

"Oheeer! Oheeer!" the trucks groaned. "We can't! We won't!"

Duck watched with interest.

Diesel lost patience. "GrrRRRrrrRRR!" he roared, and gave a great heave. The trucks jerked forward.

"Oh! Oh!" they screamed. "We can't! We *won't*!" Some of their brakes snapped and the gear jammed in the sleepers.

"GrrRRRrrrRRR!" roared Diesel.

"Ho! Ho! Ho!" chuckled Duck.

Diesel recovered and tried to push the trucks back, but they wouldn't move.

Duck ran quietly round to collect the other trucks. "Thank you for arranging these, Diesel," he said, "I must go now."

"Don't you want this lot?" asked Diesel.

"No, thank you," replied Duck.

Diesel gulped. "And I've taken all this trouble," he almost shrieked. "Why didn't you tell me?"

"You never asked me. Besides," said Duck, innocently, "you were having such fun being revo-whatever-it-was-you-said. Goodbye."

Diesel had to help the workmen clear the mess. He hated it. All the trucks were laughing and singing at him.

"Trucks are waiting in the yard;
tackling them with ease'll
'Show the world what I can do,'
gaily boasts the diesel.
In and out he creeps about,
like a big black weasel.
When he pulls the wrong trucks out
— Pop goes the Diesel!"

The song grew louder and louder and soon it echoed through the yard.

"Grrr!" growled Diesel and scuttled away to sulk in the shed.

Dirty work

Dirty work

When Duck returned, and heard the
trucks singing, he was horrified. "Shut
up!" he ordered and bumped them hard.
"I'm sorry our trucks were rude to you,
Diesel," he said.

Diesel was still furious. "It's all your
fault. You made them laugh at me."

"Nonsense," said Henry, "Duck would

never do that. We engines have our differences; but we *never* talk about them to the trucks. That would be des – des…"

"Disgraceful!" said Gordon.

"Disgusting!" put in James.

"Despicable!" finished Henry.

Diesel hated Duck. He wanted him to be sent away. So he made a plan. He was going to tell lies about Duck.

Next day he
spoke to the
trucks. "I see
you like jokes.
You made a
good joke about
me yesterday.
I laughed and
laughed. Duck told me one about Gordon.
I'll whisper it... don't tell Gordon I told
you," said Diesel and he sniggered away.

"Haw! Haw! Haw!" guffawed the
trucks. "Gordon will be cross with Duck
when he knows. Let's tell him and pay
Duck back for bumping us."

They laughed rudely at the engines as they went by. Soon Gordon, Henry and James found out why.

"Disgraceful!" said Gordon.

"Disgusting!" said James.

"Despicable!" said Henry. "We cannot allow it."

They consulted together. "Yes," they said, "he did it to us. We'll do it to him, and see how *he* likes it."

Duck was tired. The trucks had been cheeky and troublesome. He wanted a rest in the shed.

But the engines barred his way. "Hooooosh! KEEP OUT!" they hissed.

"Stop fooling," said Duck, "I'm tired."

"So are we," said the engines. "We are tired of *you*. We like Diesel. We don't like you. You tell tales about us to the trucks."

"I don't."

"You do."

"I don't."

"You do."

The Fat Controller came to stop the noise.

"Duck called me a 'galloping sausage'," spluttered Gordon.

"...rusty red scrap iron," hissed James.

"...I'm 'old square wheels'," fumed Henry.

"Well, Duck?" said the Fat Controller, trying not to laugh himself.

Duck considered. "I only wish, sir," he said gravely, "that I'd thought of those names myself. If the dome fits..."

"He made the trucks laugh at us," said the engines.

"Did you, Duck?" asked the Fat Controller.

"Certainly not, sir. No *steam* engine would be as mean as that."

Diesel lurked up. "Now, Diesel, you heard what Duck said," said the Fat Controller.

"I can't understand it, sir," said Diesel. "To think that Duck of all engines... I'm dreadfully grieved, sir, but I know nothing."

"I see," said the Fat Controller. Diesel squirmed and hoped he didn't.

"I'm sorry, Duck," said the Fat Controller, "but you must go to Edward's station for a while. I know he will be glad to see you."

"As you wish, sir," said Duck, and he trundled sadly away, while Diesel smirked with triumph.

A close shave

A close shave

Duck the Great Western Engine puffed sadly into Edward's station.

"It's not fair," he complained. "Diesel has been telling lies about me and made the Fat Controller and all the engines think I'm horrid. They think I told tales about them to the trucks and now the Fat Controller has sent me away."

Edward smiled. "I know you aren't horrid," he said, "and so does the Fat Controller, you wait and see. Why don't you help me with these trucks?"

Duck felt happier with Edward. He set to work at once and helped Edward with his trucks and coaches.

The trucks were silly, heavy and noisy. The two engines had to work hard,

pushing and pulling all afternoon. At last they reached the top of the hill.

"Peep, peep! Goodbye," whistled Duck, and rolled gently over the crossing to the other line.

Duck loved coasting down the hill, running easily with the wind whistling past. He hummed a little tune.

Suddenly he heard a whistling sound. *"Peeeeep! Peeeeep!"*

"That sounds like a guard's whistle," he thought. "But we haven't a guard."

His driver heard it too, and looked back. "Hurry, Duck, hurry!" he called urgently. "There's been a breakaway and some trucks are chasing us."

"Hurrah! Hurrah! Hurrah!" laughed the trucks. "We've broken away! We've broken away! We've broken away!"

And before the signalman could change the points they followed Duck on down the line.

"Chase him, bump him, throw him off the rails," they yelled and hurtled after Duck, bumping and swaying with ever increasing speed.

Duck raced through Edward's station, whistling furiously, but the trucks were catching up.

"As fast as we can," said the driver. "Then they'll catch us gradually." The driver was gaining control. "Another clear mile and we'll do it," he said. "Oh glory! Look at that!"

James was just pulling out on their line from the station ahead. Any minute there could be a crash!

"It's up to you now, Duck," cried the driver.

Duck put every ounce of weight and steam against the trucks. They felt his strength. "On! On!" they yelled.

"I must stop them. I *must*," cried Duck. The station came nearer and nearer. The last coach cleared the platform.

"It's too late!" Duck whistled. He felt a sudden swerve, and slid shuddering and groaning along a siding.

A barber had set up shop in a wooden shed in the siding. He was shaving a customer. There was a sliding, groaning crash, and part of the wall caved in.

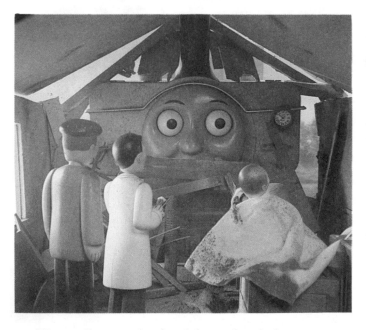

The silly trucks had knocked their guard off his van and left him far behind after he had whistled a warning.

But the trucks didn't care — they were feeling very pleased with themselves.

"Beg pardon, sir!" gasped Duck. "Excuse my intrusion."

"No, I won't!" said the barber, crossly. "You've frightened my customers and spoilt my new paint. I'll teach you." And he lathered Duck's face all over.

Poor Duck.

Thomas was helping to pull the trucks away when the Fat Controller arrived. The barber was telling the workmen what he thought.

"I do not like engines popping through my walls," he fumed. "They disturb my customers."

"I appreciate your feelings," said the

Fat Controller,
"and we'll gladly
repair the damage. But you must know
that this engine and his crew have
prevented a serious accident. You and
many others might have been badly hurt."

The Fat Controller paused impressively.
"It was a very close shave!" he said.

"Oh!" said the barber. "Oh, excuse me." He filled a basin of water to wash Duck's face.

"I'm sorry," he said. "I didn't know you were being a brave engine."

"That's all right, sir," said Duck. "I didn't know that either."

"You were very brave indeed," said the Fat Controller, kindly. "I'm very proud of you."

"Oh, sir!" sighed Duck. He felt happier than he had done for weeks.

The Fat Controller watched the rescue operation. "And when you are properly washed and mended," he said to Duck, "you are coming home."

"Home, sir?" asked Duck. "Do you mean the yard?"

"Of course," said the Fat Controller.

"But, sir, they don't like me. They like Diesel," said Duck sadly.

"Not now." The Fat Controller smiled. "I never believed Diesel," he said, "so I sent him packing. The engines are sorry and want you back."

A few days later, when he came home, there was a really rousing welcome for Duck the Great Western Engine.

· Duck ·

· Diesel ·

· Daisy ·